A colla   opinions

IN MY OWN WORDS

TREVOR SWISTCHEW

Copyright © Trevor Swistchew 2024

No part of this book may be reproduced or transmitted in any form or by any other means without permission in writing from the publisher, except by a reviewer who wishes to quote brief passages in connection with a review written for insertion in a magazine, newspaper or broadcast.

CONTENTS

Introduction 1

Thelon Z369 3

Notes From The Starfolk 11

How A.I. Will Take Over The World 15

Marxian Ideals! Sold Out! 21

Zen Story 25

Mephistopheles On Trial 35

Eve **SUES** the Dark Lord 43

The Dark Lord on Parkinson 47

Pinocchio Goes To College 55

The Fat Man and the Guitar 61

The Conversation 65

Scanaroony Tales 69

For Mr Trump 73

The Motion Picture 75

Troy Manford Will Not Be Quiet 83

Working in the Main Team 89

Letter to God (A FAIRY TALE) 95

Letter From God (ANOTHER FAIRY TALE) .. 99

Poetry 107

Freedom? 109

To Robert Burns 111

The Frustration of the Artist 112

On Being Misunderstood 114

Kye – Ho! 116

Reflection 117

To Poetry and Poets 118

Poem for a Racist 119

Social Control..121

The Quest for Innocence.................................. 123

Clarion Call 125

No Title... 126

The Heart of Mankind 127

The Vanity of Beautiful Ladies...........................128

Goodnight..130

What Every Thrill Seeker Wants....................... 132

Cash In Hand...134

Life in Thatcher's Britain 135

ABOUT THE AUTHOR 139
ACKNOWLEDGEMENTS......................... 141

INTRODUCTION

In My Own Words is a collage of stories poetry and observances of popular entrenched myths that have impacted on human thinking for thousands of years.

Trevor Swistchew a long time writer poet and enquirer offers in his own words some of his thoughts and questions into the nature of what many folk have been taught to believe.

The author points out that belief, while long established in the world, does not actually PROVE the reality of WHAT folk believe and one ought ALWAYS to question what others tell you or what you read in books or online.

Critical thinking is vital for any serious enquiry rather than just accepting what you read or see.

THELON Z369

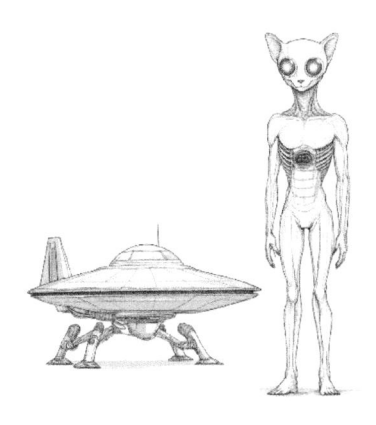

Thelon Z369—home to beings who have existed for over a million years, a civilisation so advanced that it dwarfs anything humanity has ever known. Thelonians, as we call them (though they use a name we can't even pronounce), are unlike any life forms on Earth. They appear as glassy figures, their bodies shimmering with circular lights in place of heads. They need no food, and they rarely sleep—rest for them means simply staying silent, listening to the universe.

These beings operate as one collective entity, utterly devoid of the individual ego that governs human life. Every action they take is done for the benefit of all. "Selfishness" is a concept they left behind long ago, as alien to them as their advanced science is to us. They know only peace and the endless pursuit of knowledge. Their one mission: to explore the vastness of the universe, gathering data and perfecting their sciences.

You see, long ago, they visited Earth. But when they arrived, early humans mistook them for gods. Divine beings from the stars, with knowledge of higher realms—or so the humans thought. In reality, Thelonians had no interest in spiritual enlightenment or guiding humanity. Still, they shared some of their wisdom, like how to start a fire, create the wheel, and harness water in a desert.

For almost 2,000 years, Thelonians lived among us. They were the architects of the pyramids and other wonders that modern engineers still struggle to explain. Their technology was so advanced that it seemed magical, shaping the myths and legends of the world. The gods of Norse and Greek mythology—figures like Zeus and Thor—were, in truth, aliens. They travelled unknown distances in ships that could defy gravity and the laws of physics.

Thelonians belong to a civilisation that's far beyond us on the Kardashev Scale, which measures the technological advancement of civilisations based on the energy they can harness. Type I civilisations, for example, are just slightly more advanced than humanity in 2024. But Thelonians? They're nearly one million years ahead of us. Their craft can turn invisible and make no sound—completely imperceptible to human senses.

The UFOs found on Earth, like the one in Roswell in 1947, weren't even theirs—those belonged to far less evolved beings. When Thelonians finally left Earth, they gave humanity a promise: one day, they would return. They said they would come to see how we had progressed, sparking stories of gods returning to Earth, or of a Messiah. These ideas have persisted in various forms across religions for millennia.

Thelonians are not just masters of technology; they are deeply attuned to nature. They can communicate with any life form—animal, plant, or otherwise. While on Earth, they spoke with the creatures of the oceans, learning about currents, pressure, and life beneath the waves. They learned about thermal updrafts from birds and the delicate balance of nature from the animals of the land. They saw how Earth's ecosystems were interconnected and how fragile life truly was.

In 2024, they are deeply concerned about humanity's access to nuclear weapons. They believe we are not evolved enough to possess such power, and I agree with them. Before they left, they told us that one day we would reach their level of evolution, but it would take a long, long time.

"All life evolves," they said. "Nothing remains the same. The universe itself is in constant flux." This was their parting wisdom: we cannot cling to anything—not to our lives, not to others, not even to the world as we know it. The only constant is change.

Think about that for a moment, dear reader. You and I, and everyone else, are works in progress. Everything must change. Perhaps you'd like things to stay the same forever, but that would be stagnation. Surely, what makes life unique is that it's always changing.

The Thelonians realised this truth long before humans had even discovered fire. As we continue to evolve, all the abilities they possess will naturally develop in us. This is not just speculation—it is the future of all life, not only here on Earth but in the infinite universe.

Humanity calls nature "God," but to Thelonians, nature is simply the teacher—

the universal force that guides the evolution of all life. It provides for all living things without judgement. It does not pick favourites. Nature reacts to actions and events in a way we humans interpret as "karma." The phrase "as you sow, so shall you reap" is just one of many ways we describe this universal principle.

Thelonians are not religious, but they understand the science of cause and effect and have shared this truth with other worlds they've visited. They only teach those who are ready, those whose minds are open to the reality of what they're being shown.

Some humans, even now, have glimpses of this awareness. Throughout history, there have always been individuals who seem to know things others do not. In time, all of humanity will catch up, and we too will evolve into a higher civilisation. This is certain, and it is the destiny of all life forms in the universe.

NOTES FROM THE STARFOLK

In the endless expanse of space, civilisations far beyond humanity have evolved. Type 8 civilisations, whose intelligence and technology far surpass anything on Earth, exist in realms incomprehensible to us. These beings don't need to ask questions. They can read the conscious thoughts of any life form they encounter, instantly knowing their minds. Their mission? To gather knowledge from the worlds they visit and the life forms they observe.

It is said that by the year 2224, humanity will finally reach the base level of a Type 1 civilisation. Civilisations are categorised by how much energy they can harness from their world and their sun. Type 2 civilisations can capture 100% of their sun's energy, using it to create a utopia unimaginable on Earth. Their cities, powered by unlimited energy, are designed to supply abundance for every living being. Poverty is unknown, and the need for money has been eradicated goods and services are shared freely.

The universe is constantly evolving. Civilisations rise and fall, as they have for trillions of years. Stars die, but from their destruction, new stars are born. Planets capable of supporting life emerge, continuing the endless cycle of creation. Earth, too, was once a molten sphere of matter and gas before it became home to life. This process has no end; the universe is in a state of perpetual rebirth.

Interest in Type 8 civilisations is growing rapidly among those at the forefront of science. As humanity learns more about life, the universe, and the mysteries of existence, I believe we will also learn how to cooperate—to work together for the betterment of all life. History has shown us that enlightened individuals have used their intelligence for the common good. Despite the world's challenges, there are always good people striving for progress. I trust there always will be.

Take these examples:

The Dalai Lama, a global symbol of peace and compassion.

Madam Curie, a pioneering scientist and inventor.

Andrew Carnegie, a Scottish philanthropist who gave away much of his fortune for the benefit of society.

These individuals, among others, stand as proof that humans can rise above their limitations to improve life for all. If we can continue down this path of cooperation and knowledge-sharing, who knows what the future holds? Perhaps one day we too will become a Type 8 civilisation, exploring the farthest reaches of the cosmos.

HOW A.I. WILL TAKE OVER THE WORLD

All manufacturing processes in the world operate through a series of steps, each contributing to the creation of a final product. Take, for instance, a simple cardboard box used for cereal. First, a template is made, then a machine cuts out the shape from a sheet of cardboard, before it is folded into a box. Cereal is then poured in, and the product is packed for distribution. All of these processes are completed by machines. The only human involvement is setting the controls of a computer to programme the machines.

As Artificial Intelligence (AI) advances, even this minimal human input will no longer be needed. AI will take over the programming and operation of all machinery and computers. This is why, in the near future, millions of jobs will become obsolete. Just as machines on farms replaced agricultural workers, and in coal mines where machines made miners redundant, AI will replace workers across numerous industries.

No matter how complex the processes involved in making a product, AI will be able to manage them all. From building cars to producing intricate electronics, no human input will be required. Already, we can see the groundwork for this transition.

It's important to note that many people still define themselves by what they do for work.

"Her name is Jean, she's a manager at M&S," or "he's Tom, a self-employed joiner." A job or occupation is often considered a status symbol. For years, certain professions—doctors, lawyers, and clergy—have been seen as higher-status, while shop workers and manual labourers were viewed as lower class. But in reality, this has always been nothing more than snobbery, an unfounded sense of superiority.

In any civilisation, logic tells us that all contributions are valuable to the overall good. Can anyone truly deny that all workers play a role in society's success?

The not-too-distant future will force us to confront the reality that life can no longer be defined by our jobs. Global unemployment is inevitable as industries increasingly turn to robotics and AI to meet their needs. A quick look at the jobs lost since the Industrial Revolution shows that millions of people in the UK alone have been displaced by technological progress.

Is it really necessary for everyone to have a job? Imagine a world where machines and AI produce everything required for life, allowing humanity to focus on leisure, education, and personal pursuits. If every country implemented a Universal Basic Income (UBI), people could explore the world, learn about other cultures, spend more time with their families, and pursue educational or creative interests.

There is so much to learn. The belief that people must work to be of value is outdated. If wages were replaced by a Universal Basic Income, how we view the world would change. The idea that work is essential for worth would fade, and a new understanding of life's possibilities would emerge.

In conclusion, AI is not going to stop progressing, and it will continue to take over world production. Humanity will need to accept that our involvement in these processes is becoming redundant. I see this as a positive development—a way to eliminate poverty and create a world where everyone has the freedom to explore and pursue their own interests.

MARXIAN IDEALS! SOLD OUT!

Karl Marx exposed the hypocrisy and greed that ruled the world's capitalists long before any "Revolutions" took place in China, Russia, or elsewhere. Yet replacing one economic system with another never guaranteed a fairer or happier society.

Take, for instance, Mao Tse-tung's revolution. It led to mass death and brutal repression, both in China and in Tibet. Over 40 million Chinese died in the so-called "rice famine." Local cadres, eager to make themselves look good, falsified grain storage figures. So, when the rice was desperately needed, it wasn't there.

Forty million people paid for this deceit with their lives.

In Russia, the gulags—concentration camps in all but name—were responsible for countless deaths. Human rights were entirely ignored as the regime brutally slaughtered anyone who opposed them, labelling them "counter revolutionaries". It was a convenient way of justifying mass murder.

Even today, China's leaders are too embarrassed to hold neutral talks with the Dalai Lama. They know that their only legitimacy is rooted in the threat and use of violent force. Can anyone dispute this?

Western leaders tolerate China and Russia, yet both countries are governed by men who are neither loved nor admired. These leaders are neither decent nor kind. Can anyone deny that? In Russia, Trotsky, Stalin, and Lenin all jockeyed for power, demonstrating how "revolutionary" they really were. Violence was their method of control, and Stalin, in particular, was constantly paranoid about assassination. Is that the outlook of a beloved leader?

China and Russia have tried to rewrite their countries' histories to hide their cruelty, ambition, and corruption. But the world is not as gullible as they think. In time, these leaders will face the condemnation they deserve.

To all Marxists and apologists for China and Russia, I say this: You might believe that all the cruelty and violence created better countries, but that's only because you weren't there. You didn't suffer through it.

I'm not convinced that "Revolution" serves anything other than the egos of political criminals. However, I do acknowledge that both China and Russia made significant advances in technology and greatly reduced poverty under their regimes. That much improved life in those countries.

"The Present Is All There Is."
Suzuku Roshi.

ZEN STORY

In a cave high in the Himalayas lived a Japanese Zen teacher named Suzuku Roshi. He had left Japan ten years ago to study Mahayana Buddhist teachings in India. (Mahayana means "The Broad

Path"; the "Narrow Path" is called Hinayana.)

After some time, Suzuku chose to remain in India, moving from the village he had stayed in to a cave he discovered while climbing in the mountains. The village was about three miles away and 3,000 feet lower. A round trip could take six hours or more, depending on the weather, and on many days, the journey could not be made at all. These were ideal conditions for a Zen teacher seeking a life of solitude and quiet. Suzuku could get all his provisions from the village and enjoy peace to study, write, paint, and cook.

His meals were almost entirely vegetarian—rice, root vegetables, and sometimes chicken, fish, or fruit. He wrote extensively, mostly haiku, Zen koans (short, paradoxical statements), and stories about historical teachers like

Basho and others in Zen history. His paintings followed the simple style of Japanese etchings—delicate lines on white rice paper, suggesting the subject rather than depicting it in precise detail. If you've seen traditional Japanese artwork, you'll understand this minimalist magic. If not, do look it up—it's a delight to see how a few seemingly random brushstrokes can evoke such beauty.

After a year or two in the cave, Suzuku had covered its walls with paintings of great teachers and events from the life of the historical Buddha, Siddhartha Gautama. Born a prince in India, Buddha renounced his throne to discover why life was filled with suffering and impermanence. After six years of seeking answers and studying under various teachers, Buddha realised that he had to find the truth for himself. Sitting under the Bodhi Tree—also known as the Tree of Awakening—he "awoke."

What did it mean for him to awaken? For the rest of his life, Buddha shared his insights, teaching the Dharma (Truth) selflessly to anyone who sought it. His wife became a follower, as did many of his friends. For around forty years, he turned the Wheel of Dharma, teaching until he passed into Nirvana—a state where one goes beyond suffering and rebirth.

Suzuku Roshi spent his time much like the Buddha—writing, painting, and living a contented life. He only heard about worldly matters during his trips to the village, and even then, the news was mostly local, as few villagers had the means to communicate over long distances. Eventually, technology began to infiltrate the area, and younger people started using the Internet, much like the rest of the world.

.oOo.

One day, a man and woman appeared at the cave. Suzuku was painting as they stood, panting at the entrance after their long trek up from below.

"Sir," began the man, "we ask your pardon for coming here unannounced, but we had no way of contacting you. We've heard that you are a renowned teacher in these parts and wish to meet with you, if you don't mind?"

Suzuku slowly turned his gaze toward the pair. They appeared to be in their mid-fifties, dressed in stout boots and warm clothing, with packs on their backs. Quietly stamping their feet to stimulate circulation in the cold air, they waited for his response.

"You may come in and sit," he said politely, then set aside his painting. He moved to the fire where his kettle was always ready, as Suzuku was an avid tea drinker. Gratefully, the couple looked to the kettle, clearly eager for a hot drink after their trek.

Suzuku placed a bowl on a short table, filled with rice cakes he had cooked and flavoured with honey. The cakes were light and delicious, pairing well with the tea, which was served black, without milk or sugar. In most Asian countries, milk and sugar are mainly for Western settlers, not the indigenous population. After enjoying the cakes and tea, Suzuku stood up and cleared away the dishes. He always cleaned as he went, never allowing things to pile up—a practice central to Zen teaching. Zen emphasises mindful action, treating every task as equally important. Even the smallest things matter. Do you see this, reader?

When the tea ceremony was finished (for an explanation of this wonderful Japanese tradition, look up *The Way of Tea*), the three of them began to exchange information. Genuine discussions are always about sharing knowledge.

The man introduced himself and his wife as teachers from Glasgow, Scotland. They were both Buddhist students and researchers, exploring the different traditions of Buddhism. Having come to India, the land of Buddha's birth, to study the Indian approach, they had heard of Suzuku and wanted to ask him questions to aid in their research.

Suzuku invited them to ask their questions. The woman spoke first, asking, "Is Zen teaching as true to Buddha's original teachings as other forms of Buddhism?"

Suzuku replied, "Buddha, who was fully awake, lived entirely in the present. Zen is concerned with mindfulness, so in essence, it aligns perfectly with Buddha's original Dharma teachings."

Her husband followed up with another question: "How can teachings from India and Japan be so similar?"

Suzuku explained, "The sun that shines on India is the same sun that rises in Japan every day. Buddha's teachings are universal, true for all beings, no matter where they are born or what culture they come from."

The logic of Suzuku's explanation resonated immediately with the couple, who were already familiar with Buddhist terminology and practice. They went on to ask many more questions, taking notes with Suzuku's blessing, as they were co-authoring a book on the similarities between different branches of Buddhism.

Suzuku suggested they might title their book *The Many Paths to Nirvana*. They liked the idea and did indeed use that title. In Zen, the word *Satori* has the same meaning as *Nirvana*—both denote awakening. Zen students know that *Satori* can also mean "sudden realisation," almost like a "Eureka!" moment when a question is answered and creates a feeling of elation.

Throughout all religious traditions, this sudden insight has been experienced. It shows the common thread of awakening that runs through the great spiritual teachings of the world. Suzuku Roshi knew this as a natural fact. He did not consider himself a seeker or even a teacher. He simply said, "I am awake." For those who are truly awake, there is no further inquiry needed.

The couple learned much from their meeting with Suzuku, and their book was widely read. After they returned to Glasgow, they stayed in touch with Suzuku for many years, even hosting him as a guest in Scotland. Yet, Suzuku remained in his beloved India, living in his cave, where he continued to wax like the moon until he merged with all things in the infinity of space.

MEPHISTOPHELES ON TRIAL

Finally, Satan—or Mephistopheles, to use one of his many names—stood in court, on trial for his lies and deceptions against humanity. Presiding over the case was Judge Henry Ponsonby-Snoot K.C., at the highest court in the land, the Old Bailey.

Satan had been arrested and charged after the political leaders of the world had agreed, in their desperation, that they needed a scapegoat. The world's leaders, determined to keep themselves comfortably aboard the "vote-funded gravy train," decided that to stay in power, they had to prove they genuinely cared about the masses. With violence and injustice growing rampant, the public was no longer buying their excuses. They needed someone to blame, and Satan was the perfect candidate. After all, he had been around for millennia, with a well-documented history of corrupting mankind and leading them away from the path of righteousness. What better patsy than the original corruptor from the Garden of Eden?

In the courtroom sat the jury, made up of uptight, morally superior believers, all ready to do their duty and ensure a guilty verdict. They had already decided the outcome before the trial even began. The entire process was a farce—a carefully staged performance to convince the public that justice was impartial and blind. After all, the point of this show was to protect the established elite, ensuring the politicians could remain in their cushy positions.

This trial was reminiscent of past miscarriages of justice: Hillsborough, where the police covered up their failings, leading to the deaths of innocent football fans; the Post Office scandal, where innocent employees were wrongly accused and some even took their own lives. There were also older examples, such as the betrayal of the Sepoys during British rule in India. After they were promised freedom in exchange for fighting for the British, they were rewarded instead with oppression, forcing India to fight for its independence under Gandhi.

Satan, as old as the world itself, knew all too well the wickedness of mankind. His occupation had been to tempt and deceive wherever and whenever he could. He argued that he acted only in accordance with God's will. The trial began with the prosecutor reading a summation of charges—a heavily condensed list, given that they spanned millennia. Satan had corrupted kings and peasants alike, across all lands and classes.

The prosecutor began with the names, "Lucifer Diabolicus Maximus, Nicolas Mephistopheles Sattanicas Outrageousness - hereafter referred to as Satan - you stand charged with the exclusive and wilful corruption of humanity. You are solely responsible for the current state of the world. Its injustices, its poverty, and all its suffering are your creations. How do you plead: guilty or not guilty?"

Satan looked around the courtroom, taking in the esteemed gathering of fine lords and ladies, dressed in their grand clothes, and the jury, sitting with their preconceived conclusions. He noted the members of the public on the balcony, waiting for the performance of a lifetime. Then he turned to the judge, Henry Ponsonby-Snoot K.C., and smirked. Satan knew all about the judge's penchant for cross-dressing and younger men. Inwardly, he chuckled at the court's limited powers. Even if found guilty, no sentence could ever match his deeds or undo the history of corruption he had overseen. The politicians pulling the strings from their offices had no idea what they were dealing with.

Satan calmly replied, "I am guilty of nothing other than doing God's will."

The court gasped. How could God's will involve so much suffering for mankind? The jury, full of Christian morality, was stunned.

Silence filled the courtroom as all eyes turned to the prosecutor for a response.

The prosecutor, regaining his composure, said, "You, Satan, do not follow God's will. If you did, you would be doing good."

Satan laughed out loud, causing a ripple of shock through the room. "If what you say is true," Satan responded, "then why does God allow me to continue my work? Do you, sir, know better than the Supreme Being what constitutes good or evil?"

The prosecutor paused. He had been coached on how to handle Satan's questions, but nothing could prepare him for this. Satan, unshaken and far wiser than anyone could have anticipated, continued.

"Tell me this," Satan said, addressing the court, "why does God, in all His wisdom, allow me to carry out my work? The truth is simple: I serve a purpose in God's grand design. I tempt, I deceive, but I do not act outside of His will. If mankind were pure and innocent, there would be no need for me. But as long as corruption exists in humanity, so will I."

Anger flushed the prosecutor's face. Desperate to trap Satan, he said, "You claim to do God's will, yet you offer no proof. You expect the court to believe your word, which has been corrupt since time immemorial."

Satan smiled. "You believe in God, don't you? Yet, none of you have ever seen Him. I know He is real because I was one of His first creations. I was created perfect, for God does not make mistakes. I follow only His will. If you wish to assign blame, place it on God, for He created all things, and only He knows His true purposes."

The courtroom fell into stunned silence once more. The jury, struggling to process Satan's logic, was sent out to deliberate. After over an hour, they returned with their verdict.

"Not guilty," they declared in unison.

The judge had no choice but to dismiss the case. Satan walked free, as he continues to do today, operating in the world just as he has for millennia. The verdict suited the world's leaders just fine. It kept them in power, distracted from their own failings. But with the awakening of humanity in 2024, who knows where this growing awareness will lead?

Think it over, dear reader.

EVE **SUES** THE DARK LORD

Most readers will know the story of Adam and Eve, who were said to be the first human beings, created from dust by God. But what you may not know is the tale of how Eve sued the Dark Lord after he seduced her in the Garden of Eden and left her with child.

Adam had been wandering around, marvelling at the wonders of the Garden, when he returned to find Eve in tears. Concerned, he asked her what was wrong.

Eve explained, through her sobs, that the Dark Lord had visited her while Adam was away. He had deceived her into having sex with him, claiming that his "wotsit" was the key to Paradise.

Eve fell for his lies. There was no alcohol involved, no temptation beyond his smooth words, and her virginity was stolen.

The Dark Lord, satisfied with his conquest, didn't stick around. Like many such characters, he vanished, knowing full well that the Child Support Agency would eventually come knocking for maintenance.

Eve felt utterly used and foolish, though she was far from the first of the Dark Lord's victims. Since his expulsion from Paradise, he had behaved like this - seducing, lying, and leaving destruction in his wake. It was, after all, his nature, though that's no excuse for rape in any circumstance.

Not one to accept defeat, Eve sought legal advice. Lawyers, it seems, have always existed (as long as humans have), and she found one who was more than willing to take on the case.

Eve took the Dark Lord to court to demand maintenance payments and the means to live comfortably with Adam, who was now her husband, since God had evicted them from Eden. This eviction came not only because of the rape but also because Eve had eaten the forbidden fruit from the Pink Lady apple tree - the one guaranteed to awaken cosmic awareness.

The case was a sensation. The court ruled in favour of Eve, declaring the Dark Lord to be the father of her unborn child, thanks to a DNA test that was widely reported on Jeremy Kyle's notorious television show.

The Dark Lord's legal team, unsuccessful in proving his innocence, retreated to Hell, where, naturally, they ended up running the place. After all, any lawyer worth their salt knows how to land on their feet, even in the worst circumstances.

And that, dear reader, is the *real* story of Adam and Eve. If you can believe it, you're a far better sheep than most!

Afterthought

When you think about it, Satan has fathered many children throughout history. It's logical to assume that he's the original cause behind the world's worst dictators. And, given his immortality, he always will be.

THE DARK LORD ON PARKINSON

"Good evening, viewers. In my long career in television, I have interviewed many of the world's most renowned actors, singers, and comedians. But tonight, I have the pleasure of interviewing one of the most controversial figures in history. A man of many names, whose reputation is as enigmatic as his views on life and the world. Please welcome Lucifer Diabolicus Maximus Sattanicus Nicolas Deville—known to many as the Dark Lord, or simply D.L."

Parkinson turns to the Dark Lord, seated comfortably on the couch, dressed impeccably in a tailored black suit, his aura commanding yet calm. He begins the interview.

"Your Excellency, thank you for joining us tonight and for agreeing to answer some questions that have intrigued me since my youth. When I was raised in the Church, you were always depicted as the villain. Would you like to comment on how millions of religious followers view you as the embodiment of evil?"

D.L. leans forward, his eyes gleaming with a knowing smile. "Certainly. I've always been portrayed as the antithesis of Good, and I understand why so many humans automatically see me as the epitome of wickedness. This perception comes from the lifelong conditioning they've undergone, starting in childhood, especially within organised religion. But the truth is, as an original creation of

Almighty God, I am a perfect being. You see, God is infallible—He does not make mistakes. Everything He creates is flawless, and so, in serving His divine will, I too act perfectly."

Parkinson nods, intrigued by the logic. "You explain yourself well, Your Excellency. I know that in Church teachings, we were always taught that you aimed to corrupt humanity."

The Dark Lord leans back, crossing his legs as he responds. "That's an interesting point. But here's something for you and your viewers to consider: God created humanity in His perfect image. So, how could I corrupt anyone unless they were already inclined towards corruption? Remember, all things created by a perfect God are themselves perfect, aren't they?"

Parkinson raises an eyebrow. "It's hard to argue with that kind of logic. But if what you say is true, why is there so much suffering in the world? We only need to look at the news or observe the many conflicts taking place globally."

D.L. offers a slight shrug. "From the beginning, human beings have always tried to outdo each other. It is desire and ambition, not external forces, that corrupt men. I don't actively corrupt anyone; I simply manage those who are already corrupted. My role is to keep the fallen within the Circle of Hades, to prevent their influence from spreading to the innocent and naive. Almighty God is not religious, nor does He play favourites among His creations. He is impartial, with no preference for one soul over another."

Parkinson leans forward, clearly absorbed. "That's astounding. It certainly changes how I've always thought about your role in the grand scheme of things."

D.L. smiles. "Thank you. You see, I am not inherently wicked, nor do I judge those who enter my realm. They choose their own paths. I am merely following my remit, keeping the selfish in check."

Parkinson looks thoughtful. "I was always taught that you and your followers were cast out of Paradise—evicted, if you will. Is that true?"

D.L. chuckles softly. "No, it's not true. God is perfect, as I've said before. He doesn't make mistakes, not now, not ever, and He won't in the future. So, why would a perfect Creator cast out a perfect creation from Paradise? What would be the purpose? Religion claims it was for questioning His will. But here's the fact: a perfect creation cannot question perfection. It's simply not possible. To illustrate—when you see a beautiful tree in a garden, do you attempt to improve upon it?"

Parkinson shakes his head. "No, of course not."

The Dark Lord nods. "Exactly. Now, I am not much younger than Almighty God. I figured this out trillions of years ago, and I've lived by it ever since. I don't have horns or cloven feet—those are superstitious lies, propaganda created by Church leaders to control the masses. They needed a villain to manipulate people into obedience and tithing. The idea that Almighty God requires human assistance to run the universe. Ridiculous. Yet, tragically, many still believe it."

Parkinson seems visibly impressed. "Your Excellency, I must say, your explanation is one of the clearest I've heard in a lifetime of interviewing wise men and women. Thank you for coming here tonight, and I wish you well in your future enterprises. If I should ever find myself in your domain, I hope you'll treat me kindly."

The Dark Lord offers a gracious smile. "Rest assured, Sir, you'll never enter my domain. You see, someone up there likes you. Good evening."

The audience applauds as the credits roll.

PINOCCHIO GOES TO COLLEGE

The wooden boy known throughout the world as Pinocchio, handcrafted by the puppet maker Geppetto, was finally going to college. Pinocchio had been brought to life by a kind supernatural being that humans refer to as a "fairy".

What a fairy actually is, remains unknown to mankind. The closest comparison would be to a "Jinn," often known as a "Genie" as in the tale of *Aladdin's Lamp.* Like a Jinn, a fairy can grant wishes, but these come with conditions that wise folk are wary of. There are countless stories of wishes leading to tragic outcomes. For example, the tale of a poor couple who were given three wishes, but their foolishness led to the husband finding a sausage stuck to the end of his nose. The moral of such stories is to beware of accepting gifts from strangers for nothing.

However, being quite young and not at all worldly-wise, Pinocchio set off on a particular Monday for his first day of college. He was chirpy and, after telling Geppetto to expect him home by late afternoon, skipped merrily along, singing a little song to himself:

> *"Pinocchio's going to college*
> *Gonna get some knowledge,*
> *Soon I will be smart,*
> *Then I'll have a party.*
> *Everyone can come along,*
> *Join in with my college song—*
> *Pinocchio's going to college."*

Suddenly, a well-dressed Fox stepped into Pinocchio's path from a side street. He grinned and, with a flourish of his top hat, asked, "So, you're off to college, my lad?"

Pinocchio stopped his skipping, looked the Fox up and down, noting his fancy clothes, and replied, "I certainly am, sir. I want to learn how to do things like other boys, and I want to get an education and a good job to help my grandfather, Geppetto."

"Ah," said the Fox, "Geppetto the toymaker is your grandfather, how wonderful. I know him well!" (This was a lie.) "He would be happy to know that I'll be escorting you to college, as I myself am a former student of that famous centre of learning."

"Oh, thank you, sir," said Pinocchio, naïve as ever.

.oOo.

Off they went, soon to be joined by a Weasel, who was dressed in similarly colourful clothing and spoke with the thick accent of a Cockney spiv. He approached from a nearby inn, clearly half-drunk, and began speaking:

"Ere, Guv'nor, I was just in the 'Rubber' (Cockney for 'Rub-a-dub-dub,' or pub) 'avin' a swaller when the barman points you out, comin' down the road so lively. So, I steps out to greet me old cock sparrow and his new friend!"

The Fox, who knew this Weasel all too well, was not entirely pleased to see him. He simply said, "I'm accompanying my young friend to college on behalf of my friend Geppetto. You may step along too, but mind your manners."

The Weasel looked surly but complied, knowing better than to cross the Fox.

The three of them soon arrived at the college gates, where the Fox told Pinocchio, "We'll meet again, and perhaps I'll take you to a special island where young lads get free sweets and can enjoy all the carnival shows they want."

However, Pinocchio was far wiser than the Fox realised. He had already seen some of his friends turn into donkeys after visiting such places, only to be sold into slavery. Pinocchio wasn't falling for that trick again.

.oOo.

Pinocchio succeeded in college. He worked hard, got a good job, and helped his aging grandfather, who officially adopted Pinocchio when he became a real boy.

As for Mr. Fox and the Weasel, they were both jailed for trafficking young boys and were soon forgotten by history.

(That's your lot. Goodbye!)

THE FAT MAN AND THE GUITAR

A fat man sat with an electric guitar on Rose Street, Edinburgh - Scotland's premier city, home to the Holyrood Parliament. He was singing *Rockin' in the Free World*, a Neil Young original, famously covered by bands like Krokus and Pearl Jam. Shoppers paused, drawn by the music that filled the street, pouring from a Roland 40-watt amplifier.

But where there's joy, there are always complaints. The dullards—the ones who can't stand anything but the safe, conformity-style music they grew up with—grimaced. These are the same people who've long since had their creativity stifled, taught to vote Tory or Labour, and to "keep their opinions to themselves."

"Go to work, pay your taxes, and shut it." This sentiment sums up the UK in 2024—a country that has passed laws to stifle as much "free expression" as possible. Anti-war protests are now labelled antisemitic, while the likes of Netanyahu's regime in Israel literally get away with murder. Palestine is facing genocide, and the pictures of starving, dying children stand as testimony to one Zionist liar's hunger for power. Netanyahu clings to his position, desperately avoiding prosecution for his corruption.

And what of the rest of the world's leaders? Most are too afraid to condemn the atrocities. Instead, they talk in circles, throwing out meaningless definitions and debates. Meanwhile, the carnage continues.

The American president speaks of "red lines," claiming Israel hasn't crossed any of them yet. But tell me this: if starving children aren't a red line, what exactly is?

The fat guitar player doesn't believe a word of it. And neither should you, reader—unless you've managed to suspend whatever humanity you had left after years of living in this world.

So that's it. Go and learn to *think for yourself*. The Fat Man will keep on playing until the world finally wakes up from its sleep.

THE CONVERSATION

*God in Conversation with
John E Sprokitt, Radio Presenter
on Edinburgh's Radio Blah*

John E Sprokitt: "Good evening, listeners. Welcome to tonight's *In Conversation* programme. We are privileged to have the Almighty Lord with us tonight, ready to engage in a conversation and answer the questions I've prepared on your behalf."

John turns to God, who is sitting calmly in a chair, smoking a fine Cuban cigar and enjoying a glass of Cognac.

John E Sprokitt: "Your Most High, I'd like to begin with a big question: why did you create the universe? I know it's huge, but I—and many others—really have no idea why we exist. Do you have an explanation?"

Almighty God: "Certainly, John. I know all things, being the Original Cause. Nothing is unknown to me. I created the universe out of boredom. I was alone in the vast Void of Space and decided to create companions—planets, galaxies, and other beings—for my interest and amusement."

John E Sprokitt: "Does this mean that you, Sir, are at the centre of all things in Creation?"

Almighty God: "You're sharp, young man. You've realised the truth without guidance from me. Indeed, I am all things, and all things are me. You saw this without my having to say it. Well done!"

John E Sprokitt: "Thank you! I was raised in the Church, and Jesus pointed out his Oneness with you on more than one occasion. It's entirely logical that you exist in all things. In fact, it could *not* be otherwise."

Almighty God: (Laughs) "Okay, okay. You've got the job. You can be my advocate on Earth."

John E Sprokitt: "I'm honoured, but isn't the Pope in Rome your advocate on Earth?"

Almighty God: "It may seem that way if I were a Christian, but I am beyond all religions and therefore free to choose whom I wish to represent me on Earth. Do you see?"

John E Sprokitt: "Yes, I see. Given your non-affiliation to any one faith, I understand. But do you think I'm worthy of such a role?"

Almighty God: "Of course. I don't make mistakes, and being perfect, I'm incapable of any wrong choices. So relax and enjoy your new job. You can hand in your notice to Radio Blah and come join my team—the only genuine show in town."

John E Sprokitt: "Hooray, free at last!" (John dances for joy)

John and God step into a limousine to journey to God's Offices, where only bliss awaits.

The End?

No, there will be a follow-on story about John E Sprokitt in his new role.

SCANAROONY TALES

The European Enterprise Programme (EEP) was established in the 1980s by a family of con artists from Glasgow. The scheme was simple but highly lucrative, raking in vast sums for the organisation. Operating from an office in Edinburgh, the business employed over 50 staff, offering a fail-safe way for companies to quadruple their revenue within a year.

Their pitch was a European Business Link via the Internet, providing access to all registered UK businesses within the expansive European market, boasting over 300 million potential customers. Registration cost £800 per year, and the sales team used fake "testimonials" from supposedly satisfied customers to reel in the gullible.

The sales process was straightforward. After a call handler arranged a consultation, a "Closer" from the sales team would visit the prospective client. Armed with well-organised, professional-looking literature, the Closer would convince the client that the £800 fee would guarantee the promised profits, or "your money back—no quibbles."

If the client requested tangible proof, they were shown glowing testimonials from fake clients. If they pushed further, they were given the phone number of a major international business. When the number was called, the enquiry was automatically diverted to the Edinburgh office, where one "Martin Adams" would pose as an executive for the supposed business. It worked like a charm. One Closer was overheard saying, "This is a great job. You talk rubbish for 20 minutes and earn over £300 in commission."

The office staff and sales team were highly motivated and earned good money for selling a non-existent service. The whole operation was cheap to run and could be managed from a modest-sized office. The enterprise regularly changed locations, especially after operating in one area for over a year and when businesses began realising that their promised profits had failed to materialise.

When the jig was up in one place, the offices simply vanished, reopening under a different name in a new location, where they continued to exploit the natural greed of those who believed that money could grow on trees.

Most of the team eventually realised that the entire operation was a scam. However, the financial rewards were so good that their greed overtook any sense of fairness they might once have had. I write this story from personal experience, as a former employee who discovered that I had been working for a fraudulent organisation. I left the company and later learned that they had relocated to London.

They actually called me and offered me another job. I'm happy to say I declined.

My advice to readers? If anyone offers you a deal like this, think long and hard before paying any fees. Remember the old adage: "If an offer sounds too good to be true, it probably is."

(Excelsior.)

FOR MR TRUMP

(This song is sung to the tune of 'These books are made from walking' by Nancy Sinatra)

You keep saying,
you got somethin' for me.
Somethin' you call hope,
I must confess
You are just so full of phoney bullshit,
and only you is getting' all your best

These boots are made for kickin'
an' that's just what they'll do
One of these days –
Boots'll kick the crap right out of you.

An' you keep lyin'
when you oughtta be truthin,
And you keep thinkin
that you ain't never getting' exposed.

Well, you should know
I ain't no patsy,
An' I'll kick your ass
right down your lyin' road.

An' you keep bettin'
when you oughtta be quittin'
And you republicans
think you're God's gift to the world
But you are just a crowd
of Right-wing Liars
An' it's into political oblivion
you'll be hurled.

THE MOTION PICTURE

Tony Swan knew all too well about child abuse. He had over ten years' experience of the "care system" and even in his 70s was still feeling the impact. After being placed in six Children's Homes where abuse was rife, he well knew that predators had infested the system in numbers to carry out their nefarious activities using vulnerable children to sate their heinous lusts. Tony could write reams of data on the many abusers he had encountered, whose filthy language had terrified his young mind when he was a child.

.oOo.

It all started when he was six years old in a Care Home in Scotland, where an abusive and tyrannical "Matron" dominated the young folk in her care in ways that were certainly NOT in keeping with what her mouth said. All lovey-dovey for Visitors, until they left, then her real self emerged. From insults to assaults, then regular beatings, and the unwanted attention of predators.

Tony, even at a young age, was well aware of things that no child should know. Even after he and his brother and sister got home, the impact remained to remind them all that adults are not trustworthy. This, of course, tainted them for life.

For Tony it did not end there; he went to a further five care homes, where the abuse continued like an unwelcome thread through his life.

It was only when he was sixteen and a half when the care abuse stopped, though further abuse did not.

In a few of his jobs predatorial men homed in on him, perhaps sensing his vulnerable nature. I think that children who are abused somehow transmit a weakness to predators who then target those young folks as though they are lawful prey.

As Tony grew older, he had analysed himself many times and had listened to councillors and written his story into a book and sent it out to anyone who showed any interest in Child Protection. One might think EVERYONE would want to know, yet often editors of newspapers Tony approached were almost reluctant to review his work, or even advertise it.

Tony figured they saw it as embarrassing, yet his experience qualified his criticism of the system, that for probably centuries and turned a blind eye to the abuse of hundreds of thousands of children, not only in Care Homes, but in Private Schools too.

Indeed, the world-famous school attended by Royalty had recently been slated in an official Report showing that Child Abuse is Universal wherever young folk are gathered in large numbers. The Church itself is involved, and the film "SPOTLIGHT" showed the worldwide scale of child abuse perpetuated by priests and nuns of the Catholic and other Christian organisations.

The coverup raised a stink to heaven and was exposed by the BOSTON GLOBE newspaper.

In Rome, the Pope removed an offending Cardinal (Law) and appointed him to a very senior post in the Vatican, saying that he (The Pope) was "hurt" by the allegations, though not one word of empathy for the abused children that Cardinal Law had targeted. Hypocrisy or what?

Tony knew many other survivors, who like him had known the hard truth of life in Care. He was determined to reach out to as many as he could to share his story, which he had published as a book, "KNOCKING DOWN THE WALL." It was online at Amazon and Kindle, and he had already sent free copies to many outlets to gain a following, who in turn would promote his work.

Tony had tried to look at the International Impact of Child Abuse, not only the lifelong impact and emotional and financial damage, but the cost also internationally to world economies.

In America alone, the financial impact of child abuse was reckoned by some to exceed 12 Trillion Dollars lost to America's economy through the hundreds of thousands of victims who were impacted emotionally and could not work regularly, if at all.

Then there was the cost of counselling and drug therapies that many were in need of. Finally, the calculated figure included the lost taxation caused through many of the survivors not having the capacity to work and therefore pay tax. One must also include the many lawsuits and court settlements that also cost the economy billions of dollars. To add to these huge costs, there were also the costs of imprisoning predators, often for years, and that loss of revenue to the economy.

For example, in the UK the cost of one prisoner per week in prison is around £2,000. Yearly that rises to over £25,000.

In Edinburgh's Saughton Prison in 2024 there were around 60 predators resident. The net cost to The State was £1.5 MILLION POUNDS PER YEAR.

Now, collectively, anyone who does the math can see at once why child abuse is so awful, not only through the pain it causes to individual children, but the ongoing unending costs to the country they live in.

It follows that IF all Child Abuse were stopped, far more of the taxpayers' money would be freed up to address other social issues, and one must also consider the better lives of all children.

Realistically though, predators are *NOT* going to stop abusing children. Although one thinks it would be wonderful to see all abuse stop, it simply won't. Therefore, the best anyone can try to do is limit the opportunities that those who target children have and do everything possible to curtail abuse.

I have written lists of ways I think would help prevent abuse, but these have yet to be implemented.

From bracelets for children linked to the Police, to predators permanently wearing a tag, to stricter sentencing, as well as (wherever feasible) convicted predators paying cash compensation to their victims.

Predators do not stop, they are only stopped by being caught and jailed, or when they die. This being so, and given the fact that Child Abuse is Universal, one can only continue to campaign to raise awareness and try to create a mindset in the public that demands an all-out end to Child Abuse.

TROY MANFORD WILL NOT BE QUIET

Troy Manford knew that aliens had long been in contact with scientists and key figures at NASA. Ever since the Roswell crash in 1947, where newspapers initially reported a "flying disc" had been recovered along with several alien life forms—both living and dead—Troy had immersed himself in studying everything he could about the incident. He believed that if the truth were ever fully known, it would change humanity's understanding of itself and the universe.

He saw how quickly the American political machine had pressured newspapers to alter the original story, replacing "flying disc" with "weather balloon," while all notes on alien life forms were quietly buried. This cover-up fed into the many conspiracy theories circulating in America and around the world, but Troy wasn't swayed by theories alone. He had questions, and he was determined to find answers.

Troy was well aware of *Area 51*, a top-secret military base in Arizona where UFOs and alleged alien beings were taken for examination. Many books spoke of cover-ups, international rivalry, and the desire of superpower nations to monopolise alien technology in order to gain an advantage over their rivals. For Troy, it was more than just a political game. The truth about extraterrestrial life had implications for the entire human race, challenging long-held beliefs about humanity's place in the universe.

.oOo.

Troy had spoken to numerous military personnel and scientists who claimed to have had direct contact with alien beings. These beings, originating from other galaxies, were curious about Earth, just as humans are curious about other worlds. They had been visiting Earth for thousands of years, influencing human history by sharing their technological expertise with early civilisations. Aliens were said to have played key roles in the discovery of fire, the invention of the wheel, and the construction of ancient buildings. Early humans, in awe of their advanced capabilities, often mistook these beings for gods, referring to them as "star people."

But these visitors weren't divine. They were simply evolved life forms, much like humanity, only far more advanced. The encounters between humans and these beings formed the basis of many religious ideas, which were born out of ignorance and awe at these initial meetings. Belief in the superiority of these extraterrestrials was a common misconception. Truly enlightened beings understood that this was an illusion, founded on the misunderstanding that evolved technology was the same as divine power.

.oOo.

Troy was determined to expose the truth about aliens on Earth. He believed that they were being manipulated by powerful men whose only interests were money and control. Meanwhile, the alien agenda seemed to be focused on gathering data and guiding humanity, particularly regarding the use of nuclear weapons. In other galaxies, planets had destroyed themselves through the misuse of nuclear weapons, and many advanced alien civilisations were aware of just how dangerous these technologies could be. It was part of their mission to warn developing civilisations, like Earth, about the catastrophic potential of nuclear arms.

What most people didn't know, Troy argued, was that an intergalactic federation existed. This federation was dedicated to sharing knowledge across galaxies, helping to awaken life forms to the critical need for caution with nuclear technology. Those humans who had directly encountered advanced alien life had yet to fully grasp what they were dealing with. Troy believed that the matter was far too important to be left in the hands of men who couldn't comprehend the urgency of their universal responsibility to humanity.

Troy Manford wasn't going to stay silent, and this story is just one of his many attempts to spread the truth, urging humanity to uncover the facts for themselves.

Troy Manford is not his real name, nor is his location known. His mission is to expose the suppression of information and infiltrate human consciousness with the knowledge that aliens are real—and that many of the world's military and political leaders already know this as fact.

Enough said for now. Troy Manford will return.

WORKING IN THE MAIN TEAM

John was loving his new job. He had been hired by God after interviewing Him on one of his shows on *Radio Blah*. John's sharp wit had impressed the Original Creator, who then offered him a prestigious position on His team.

John's new role was as Director of Communications, a title that made him the bridge between God's plans for humanity and the task of informing said humanity of these divine designs. On the door of his plush office was a brass plaque that read:

MR. J.E. SPROKITT,
Director of Communications

The office itself exuded prestige, with oak panelling, a mahogany desk, and a leather chair. A computer sat on the desk, alongside a liquid lamp meant for relaxation. The soft background music added little to the room's function, but its presence gave the impression of high status to any visitor.

Many jobs in communications seem undefined, and many people who work in the field don't know how to communicate. Often, they appear to invent things as they go along—something that, in truth, is accurate for many. John, however, was a communicator, able to distil complex issues into simple words, conveying his meaning with precision through either the written or spoken word. He was the perfect appointee. After all, God cannot err, and John was expected to perform correctly in all situations, as God already knew, being able to see into the future to infinity and beyond.

.oOo.

During his first few days, John was briefed on his role and responsibilities. He would interview famous leaders, both from history and the present day, and gather data that would determine their future and liabilities for their past actions, all in line with the Universal Law of Karma. However, John soon learned that the job was not as straightforward as it seemed. He had to decide on outcomes and the appropriate retributions for the karmic consequences incurred by those he judged, all under God's direction.

Some might argue that John couldn't possibly make mistakes, as the Perfect, All-Wise God, would direct his every move. In this sense, John might be seen as merely a puppet, with his decisions already preordained. Yet, this was not clear to John, who often fretted over the fate of his "clients."

Despite the challenges, the pay was excellent, and the perks were far superior to anything he had experienced in his previous role at *Radio Blah*.

.oOo.

After a few weeks, John became familiar with the daily routines, meetings, and schedules that took him to world-famous cities. There, he met with dignitaries, politicians, lawyers, clergy, and foreign emissaries who were ambitious and keen to maintain their positions of power and privilege. These people were far more ambitious than John had ever imagined, having realised long ago how cushy their lives could be by conforming to the nonsense they heard and by keeping their feet firmly planted under fortune's bountiful table.

John, however, had no interest in that. His focus was solely on determining their guilt and recommending the appropriate retribution. He reported directly to God, who often pretended to be astonished by John's findings, even though, of course, God already knew everything John would say. After all, a Cosmic, Eternal, All-Knowing Deity cannot not know anything and is always seeking new ways to add a little diversity to the story of creation, if only to keep things interesting.

God's boredom was the real challenge here. Even before creating anything, He already knew how it would turn out. The only way for Him to escape such omniscient tedium was to wilfully forget

Himself and play the roles of existence as if He were not God. Consider, for a moment, that the historical story of Creation was no mystery to Him, nor were any of its outcomes.

Imagine if you were responsible for everything.

.oOo.

Until you fully awaken, life is really just a dream.

LETTER TO GOD
(A FAIRY TALE)

Almighty originator of all things, this letter embodies many of the questions that have intrigued me since birth.

My nature compels me to question everything, pushing me to probe the ideals and rituals that humanity has followed for millennia, in an effort to unravel their origins. I believe this exploration will open my eyes to life and the true nature of all things.

I write to you as the Primal Force that caused the entire universe to manifest, hoping that you will consider answering my questions. I seek peace from my endless inquiries. I understand that you receive similar questions from many others and that you've likely had countless requests for the inside scoop. I do not know how many have received their answers, but it seems logical to assume that the quest for understanding never truly ends.

Nevertheless, I am compelled to ask my own questions. I cannot accept that others' inquiries will satisfy my personal search. Each life, I realise, is a separate journey, even though all beings originate from the same source, which humanity has named "God."

Now to my questions:
- Why did you create a universe with so much suffering?
- Why are there wars?
- Why are people excessively violent and cruel to one another?

- Why do some humans believe they have the right to impose laws on others, without regard for how those laws impact the lives of those being targeted, especially by would-be dictators?

I could ask many more questions about what I have witnessed in the world or experienced since birth, but I believe that if I had answers to just these few, they might address the others in part.

So, may I kindly ask that you answer what I've posed for now?

Yours most affectionately,

A.N. Enquirer

LETTER FROM GOD (ANOTHER FAIRY TALE)

Dear Mr. Enquirer,

Our Enquiry Office received your letter, along with trillions of others from across the universe. Due to the sheer volume of correspondence sent to this office, responses take considerable time to reach those who write in. I kindly ask for your patience as your questions are addressed.

You'll appreciate that the Most High does not read every letter personally. The number of enquiries requires a full staff and sorting team just to categorise them, distinguishing between serious questions and those that are whimsical or mere religious propaganda, which we receive quite frequently.

Your letter poses serious questions and has been forwarded to our Logical and Reason Officers for response. In time, you will receive an official reply addressing your questions.

We acknowledge the interesting premises in your letter. This office ever dismisses no question, and we treat all enquiries with due compassion and regard.

Thank you for writing. Your reply will follow in due course.

Initial Response Team
Office of the Most High

.oOo.

Dear Mr. Enquirer,

Further to our initial reply, here is the final response to your questions, which I have listed numerically for clarity.

Your replies are as follows:

1. **Why does the universe have so much suffering?**

   The universe was the original manifestation of God. Suffering is a necessary part of existence in all physical forms and cannot be entirely avoided. Even the greatest saints in the history of Earth and other worlds have endured suffering throughout time and space.

   For example, Lord Jesus suffered death on the cross. His divinity did not prevent him from suffering. However, he bore it without complaint. This doesn't mean suffering doesn't matter—it means how one relates to suffering shapes one's perception of it. Ageing, for example, involves inevitable suffering as the body grows old and weakens. Similarly, lack of food leads to hunger, and lack of water causes thirst. These forms of suffering are real, albeit relatively minor.

You may ask why suffering exists at all. The answer is that it is unavoidable in certain circumstances. Complaining about suffering serves no purpose because, without it, humanity would not learn lessons of real value. While this may seem strange, upon reflection, you will come to realise that suffering has its own value, even if it is unwelcome.

Finally, you should consider that much of human suffering is self-inflicted by the way people live their lives. For instance, people smoke despite knowing that it causes illness, or they abuse drugs and alcohol, leading to further suffering. The universe, or God, does not impose suffering on humanity—most of it stems from individuals' own actions. I do not expect you to accept this answer immediately; I invite you to reflect on it and form your own understanding.

2. **Why are there wars?**
   This is a complex question that has its roots in the male ego. Throughout millennia, men have sought to own land, control natural resources, and dominate others, which breeds resentment and leads to war. In essence, wars arise when old men entrenched in power send young men to die to protect their assets.

You may ask if there has ever been a just war—a war fought to liberate people or to share the Earth's natural wealth for the common good, as intended by God. The great sages of every religion have taught this principle, yet it is often ignored, leading to wars, whether local or global, such as the world wars of history.

The simple answer to war is peace, though it may seem naïve. It is for humanity to reflect on this if war is ever to end.

3. **Why are some human beings excessively cruel and violent?**

Some individuals grow into adulthood without any moral compass, guidance, or awareness of how their actions affect others. This leads them to behave cruelly or violently, with little thought to the consequences for those around them.

4. **Why do some human beings impose laws without regard for others?**

   This stems from a desire to control others and accumulate power, often at the expense of the very people such laws are meant to govern. The result is a world where dictators and oppressive regimes flourish, disregarding the well-being of those they rule.

   .oOo.

We hope these answers provide some clarity to your queries. Reflect on them, and may you find peace.

Yours sincerely,
Office of the Most High

POETRY

FREEDOM?

Pissed as a newt
Judas confessed
that he tipped off the Romans
that Night.
Jesus got done
in Gethsemane Garden
the Romans were just too uptight
Huge jaggy bonnet
stuck on his scalp,
whipped up a hill with a cross
The Crucified man, committed
no crime,
His death was Humanity's loss.
Yet three days later,
He rose again,
to baffle the Romans and show,
The righteous are saved

from Death's scary jaws
and freed from this Kingdom below.
If you get the point
and you feel the truth
then turn from all your wicked ways
and you will be known
as a light for the world
and live without hate
all your days.

TO ROBERT BURNS

He had a heart,
there's no denying
He was a lad, forever trying
To show a truthful view of life
With all its pain and love and strife

Jean Armour was his treasured lass
Sweet words to her old Rab did pass
And though other women
caught his 'een'
Auld Rabbie was fair stuck on Jean.

His fame has spread
all round the earth
From Nova Scotia up to Perth
His life, well lived,
will never end
Toast Robert Burns,
all mankind's friend

THE FRUSTRATION OF THE ARTIST

The yearning to be understood
And not be merely seen as crude
For painting pictures in the nude
Which some folk think is very good

The artist paints, and with each stroke
Of brush, depicts weight of life's yoke
The pan of ordinary folk
Who live life hard, it is no joke

Some people think his work a waste
And oft condemn it in their haste
But artists, working with life's "paste"
Have sensed a life that few can taste

The humanness which drives them on
And bides them work from dusk 'til dawn
Shows mankind's spirit has not gone
And shows that Joy has not yet flown

We are all artists in our heart
And love is where we make a start.
Some minds would like to break apart
"It's good," they say, "but is it Art?"

ON BEING MISUNDERSTOOD

Caution is the operative word
If one wishes to be heard
And not have one's speech soundly blurred
Or have one's meaning quickly slurred
By people with whom one converses
While sitting quietly on our 'erses
And eating cakes and drinking tea
This makes for pleasing company.

A word or two quietly said
With care and taste will reach the head
The brainbox of the other party
So mind and say naught that is clarty,
Especially when engaged in drink
For that can alter the way we think
And drinking, that which doth ferment
Can quickly lead to argument.

In conclusion may I say
That silence is the proper way
To pass the message properly
The less you speak, the more you say.

KYE – HO!

Through all these lands
Let the true warrior spirit arise!
The warriorship that defeats
Delusion, ignorance and aggression
Mankind's true "enemies"
Externalised as "other" in our ignorance
May the teaching of Milarepa the
Renunciate
Open the Eye of Wisdom
In all beings.

The sun arose at midnight
The Doors of Perception were cleansed
And the scheme of things
Seen clearly
For the first time.

(*Kye – Ho is a Tibetan expression meaning "Awake" or "Attention")

REFLECTION

Within the walls of memory
The shadows of the past
I walk outside, looking out,
The world is changing fast
From early years, 'til present day
The reactive painful view
That lingers on, like frozen rain
Touching all that I must do
Communicating what it is
No easy task I see
For each must walk in their own shoes
Until they can be free
The words on paper can't transmit
Except in clumsy way
What one wants to articulate
To melt the past away.

TO POETRY AND POETS

If there is something to be said
It will speak itself
If there is something to be written
It will write itself

I am no poet
And if I am
The poetry is not mine.

POEM FOR A RACIST

Hey! Racist
When you wake up in the morning
And turn on your Japanese radio
to listen to music
Played by people from all over the world
And drink your tea from China
Or coffee from Brazil
Before putting on your American jeans
And cotton clothes made in India
Consider the question
Why am I a racist?

When you go to see your football team
Most of whose players are foreign
Owned perhaps by a Russian oligarch
Wearing your scarf made in India
Consider the question
Why am I a racist?

Getting into your German designed car
Fuelled by oil from Saudi Arabia
Built by Eastern Europeans
And go to an American company
For a burger
Consider the question
Why am I a racist?

Then understand that everything you eat, wear or use is made through the cooperation of many other people, mostly those you are racist towards.

Are you still a racist?

SOCIAL CONTROL

Try to detect yourself
A hint of sadness
Over what might have been.
They, the boss figures expect too much
They said they require "indicators"
But really it's another way of saying
"If your face fits …!"

Police	]	
Education	]	
Morals	] - Means of social
Values	] control
Parents	]	

The Future, it all lies in the Future
This is no way to run a planet
The system is corrupt - only –
We don't have a system
Just a bloody shambles.

The worst has already happened
Now its time to clear up the mess
And it won't be done by force
People can only be human
When they know how to love.

THE QUEST FOR INNOCENCE

Where have you brought me to life?
What is this place?
By god, I've read the history books,
a catalogue of despair, death,
and suffering.
Why do we exist? Where are we
and where are we going?
Do we live merely to die?
To wander aimlessly, seeking pleasure
And avoiding pain,
wherever we may find it?
There are those who wallow in pleasure
There are those who wallow in pain
There are people spouting truths
Politicians lying through their teeth.

What is this, this existence,
which marks everyone

Who is born into this plane of existence?
I must come back to myself
for some kind of reference
For I trust no one.

I love

My love is fragmented
Emotions crash and thunder
within our flesh form
Mind is full of wonder,
puzzlement, question, doubt
Sometimes content to just observe.

To look without naming what we see
And to see what exists,
without language
Without labels attaching themselves
To see the world with innocent eyes!

CLARION CALL

Society listen
You educate our people
Exercise social control
Then you tell us that animals
Ain't got no soul
There ain't no sense in you
Yet you claim to be right
You're so mixed up
You ain't never seen the light
Your armies and your navies
And your air force too
Will be of little use
When Brother Death calls on you
You think death is an enemy
But death is a friend
You'll see Death in the beginning
'cause Death ain't the end.

NO TITLE

Propagate self
Life after life
Impulse to be
Give rise to
Birth in form
Lifetime after lifetime
The quest to satisfy
Desire of all kind
The procreation of beings
The agony and the ecstasy
Continues
On and on after life goes
Rippling
Like waves overlapping
Needless suffering
If only we could see

THE HEART OF MANKIND

The heart of mankind
Bleeds for you
And bleeds for me
The bleeding is compassion
Is truth, - Is our salvation
Yours and mine
And all of us.

The tears of Mankind
Fall for you
And fall for me
The falling of tears
Is compassion, is truth
Is our salvation
Yours
And mine
And all of us.

THE VANITY OF BEAUTIFUL LADIES

"Mirror, mirror on the wall!
Who is the fairest of us all?"
The wicked Queen's voice rang out.
Self-praise is no honour,
there's no doubt.

The voice replied, "My Queen, my Queen
You've asked me that for many years.
Thinkest thou that beauty forever lasts?
No point in yearning for the Bird of Youth
Or shedding tears.
For all grow old and all must die.
Think you that beauty may forever lie
With only you, and with none other?
My Queen, wake up and me,
never bother!
The world is full of people whom

Imagine their youth always abloom.
Who live in the realm of self-deceit
Regarding looks from head to feet.
True beauty lies in being true.
That beauty lies inside of you.
No make-up, or treatment,
beauty can stay
The Bird of Youth must fly away.
Now meditate upon this advice
Which at first glance may sound not nice,
If, growing old, no-one would allow,
We'd all be packed like sardines by now!"

GOODNIGHT

I close my eyes
I close my ears
I close my mouth
To this world.

Everything switches off!

And I become aware
Of another reality
A reality within
A reality which is inside and outside.

A world of quiet and silence and dark,
deep dark.
I carry it around with me
It is part of my being
I am part of my being.

There's nothing to depend on
There's nobody to lean on
In this, or any world.
We have to rely on ourselves
That's really how it is.

Goodnight!

WHAT EVERY THRILL SEEKER WANTS

A massive cash injection
A big pad by the sea
A bloody good job with "prospects"
Red wine and loads of brie.

A fuel injected Volvo
To park outside the shop
A holiday home in Corfu
A real good disco hop.

A nubile to hold on to
Lovely sunny tan
Woolwich interest regular
A townhouse in Tokyo, Japan.

The finest clothes from Austi Reed
And dinner at the "George"

The "Rolls" of course to take one there
    To laugh and drink and gorge.

Yes, these are the things that most want
    Cause we ain't no bloody fools
We'll have them yet, just wait, you'll see
    The day we win the "Pools"

CASH IN HAND

SONG BY (RAW POWER)

Welcome to the yahoo age
Sweating out ya guts for a living wage
Pay ya bills and don't complain
We got money on the brain
We got banks and ain't it grand
Much dough yeah cash in hand
Mr Big Shot don't ya understand
Open the doors we got cash in hand
Money buys and ya dreams
Money don't just talk – it screams
Folding banknotes crispy clean
Loads of dosh it's just obscene
Add it up an' pile it high,
build a bankroll in the sky
Mr Big Shot don't ya understand
Open the doors we got cash in hand

LIFE IN THATCHER'S BRITAIN

(PARODY IN A PENSIONER'S MOOD)

Och Jesus! Michty me, can it be true?
That they are sellin' aff the watter noo
The advertisin's been on my teevee
They're tryin' tae bump oot shares
   tae you an' me.

Noo ah wis aught that rain
   fell frae the sky
Nae charge wis pit on it by God, foreby
But greedy human beings seek to price
The watter which ah dinnae think
   is very nice.

They want tae line their pockets oot o' us
They say we shouldnae mak a lot o' fuss
Efter a' they've pit
   their capital intae plant
And even under pressure winnae recant.

But dinnae be amazed, it's nae mystery
There's ay been sell-offs,
throughout history
Fae 'clearances' tae coal,
it's pretty plain
Resources hae been flogged,
then flogged again.

Humans hae traded
in baith meat and men
Black people selt for slavery, and then
Of coorse, deep doon
we ken it wisnae recht
But bisiness must continue,
cash is techt.

The poll tax, there's anither load o' piss
It's sad that life should
hiv tae come tae this
That everyone should pay
exact the same

Wi' scant regard tae income,
whit a game.

But wait! There is a remedy at hand
Tae oust thon tyrant Thatcher
fae oor land
The nation needs tae vote t'ither way
An' Thatcherist ideals will cease … today!

I ken you've had aboot enough
O' me an' all this literary stuff
Please dinnae say tae me that life's unfair
For if 'they' could
'they'd' tak the very air
But freends, that is anither story
An' don't blame me,
I've nivir voted Tory!
*(This poem was written when Iron Maggie
was Prime Minister, and dates from 1982)*

ABOUT THE AUTHOR

If you liked this book, please put a review on Amazon or Goodreads for it as it really helps encourage others to read it too. And if you like my writing, I also wrote *Knocking Down the Wall*, a profound two-part memoir that explores the depths of childhood trauma and the relentless pursuit of healing. This was published in 2024 with the help of The Book Whisperers.

www.amazon.co.uk/dp/B0D5MHR7XB

Trevor Swistchew writes songs as well as playing guitar and recording his own material. He has written other works as well as poetry books and has written many thousands of letters to newspapers and publications throughout the world. He is currently promoting his new writing online.

For information Google *Trevor Swistchew Knocking Down The Wall*.

Any comments on In My Own Words email t.swistchew65@gmail.com

Thank You For Reading This.

ACKNOWLEDGEMENTS

I'd like to extend my heartfelt thanks to Mary Turner Thomson and her colleagues at The Book Whisperers for their invaluable help in bringing this next work, *In My Own Words*, to publication. This collection of short stories and poetry is something I hope readers will enjoy.

A special thank you goes to Future Pathways for help with this project, and to John Crawford, who always encourages positive endeavours.

I'm also grateful to everyone who suggested ideas or additions - your input means a great deal.

I'm already working on more projects for future collections, and to all who take the time to read my work, you mean the world to this artist, who has learned, to some degree, to laugh at himself. From my early works like *The Unemployed Person's Guide to Edinburgh* and various collections of comic verse, to my ongoing writing as a way to communicate ideas - well, as they say, the beat goes on.

Printed in Great Britain
by Amazon